# The Adventures of MARY-KATE & ASHLEY™

## THE CASE OF THE

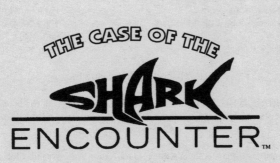

# SHARK ENCOUNTER™

A novelization by Nancy E. Krulik

WILL SOLVE ANY CRIME BY DINNER TIME™

DUALSTAR PUBLICATIONS          PARACHUTE PRESS, INC.

## SCHOLASTIC INC.

New York    Toronto    London    Auckland    Sydney

DUALSTAR PUBLICATIONS     PARACHUTE PRESS, INC.

Dualstar Publications
c/o 10100 Santa Monica Blvd.
Suite 2200
Los Angeles, CA 90067

Parachute Press, Inc.
156 Fifth Avenue
Suite 325
New York, NY 10010

Published by Scholastic Inc.

With special thanks to Robert Thorne and Harold Weitzberg.

Printed in the U.S.A.
February 1997
ISBN: 0-590-88010-1
A B C D E F G H I J

# Ready for Adventure?

It was the best of times. It was the worst of times. Actually it was bedtime when our great-grandmother would read us stories of mystery and suspense. It was then that we decided to be detectives.

The story you are about to read is one of the cases from the files of the Olsen and Olsen Mystery Agency. We call it *The Case Of The Shark Encounter.*

It was a really tough case to solve—filled with real-life pirates, a crazy mixed-up code, and dangerous sharks.

But we weren't afraid to dive right in. Because we always live up to our motto: Will Solve Any Crime By Dinner Time!

# Chapter 1

"Mary-Kate, look!" Ashley cried. "Our detective stand is still here!"

"I had a hunch it would be," I said.

Ashley raced toward our detective stand, right in the middle of Sea World. Sea World is a marine-life park in Orlando, Florida. It's filled with birds, dolphins, whales, fish—even turtles. It's a great place to visit...and an even better place to solve mysteries!

I'm Mary-Kate Olsen. My twin sister, Ashley, and I are the Trenchcoat Twins. We love solving mysteries. We're detectives!

Usually we do our detective work in our office. It's in the attic of our house in California. But today we were at Sea World with our parents.

Mom and Dad are computer geniuses. Last year, they came to Sea World to write a computer program that helps people work with dolphins.

Now Sea World needed them back to fix a problem with the computer program. And we got to come along!

"Last one to the stand is a rotten egg!" Ashley called over her shoulder as she ran.

"Woof!" Clue barked.

Clue is our brown-and-white basset hound. She has floppy ears and a big, wet nose—perfect for sniffing out clues. We call her our silent partner. She helps us solve mysteries.

Ashley, Clue, and I reached the detective stand at the exact same second.

Then we both started to laugh. Sometimes we do things exactly alike. That might be because we're twins.

We're both nine years old. We both have strawberry blond hair and big blue eyes. We look alike, but most of the time, we don't act alike—or even think alike!

Ashley thinks and thinks about every problem. And then she thinks some more. Not me. I work on hunches. I always want to jump right in!

"I wish we could jump right into a new case," I told Ashley.

"Don't worry, Mary-Kate," Ashley said. "We'll find a mystery as soon as people see that we're open for business." She pointed to the sign across the top of our stand. It said:

MARY-KATE & ASHLEY—DETECTIVES
WILL SOLVE ANY CRIME
BY DINNER TIME

"Excuse me," a deep voice boomed out. "I have a mystery for you to solve."

*Hooray!*

Ashley and I turned around—and came face to face with a chubby man. He had a thick mustache and graying hair.

"Mr. Kramer!" we both said at once. We

each gave him a big hug.

Mr. Kramer is the manager of Sea World. He's in charge of *everything*. We met him the first time we were at the park.

"I brought your detective stand out of storage," Mr. Kramer told us. "I wanted it ready for your next big mystery."

I pulled my detective notebook out of my backpack. Our great-grandmother Olive gave us both notebooks. Great-grandma Olive loves mysteries. She taught us that good detectives keep their notebooks ready at all times.

"So, what's the mystery?" I asked.

Mr. Kramer grinned. "I'd like to know, where are the two lips in tulips?" he joked.

Ashley groaned.

"Don't you have a *real* mystery for us?" she asked.

"Nope. There's nothing fishy here at Sea World," Mr. Kramer replied.

Now I groaned. Not *another* bad joke!

*Beep! Beep!*

"That's my beeper." Mr. Kramer looked at it and frowned. "Someone needs me at our shark exhibit, Terrors of the Deep. I can't imagine why." He hurried away.

We sat down behind our detective stand.

"Now what do we do?" Ashley asked.

"Now we wait for a mystery," I answered.

A family walked by our detective stand. "Hey, look—twin detectives," the little boy said to his parents. "Maybe they can answer my question."

"I don't think so," his mother said. "We need an expert to answer this question."

I stood up. "Excuse me," I called to the mother. "My sister and I have solved some very important mysteries. We know the answers to *a lot* of tough questions."

"Right," Ashley added. "And we might even know an expert who can help you."

The father stepped up to our stand. "Do you know any ichthyologists?" he asked.

"What's an ik-thee-ol-o-jist?" I asked back.

"A fish expert," the father told us.

"That's who we need," the mother said. "Because only a fish expert could explain what we just heard."

"What did you hear?" I asked.

"Singing sharks!" the little boy said.

*Singing sharks?*

"I never heard of *any* singing fish," Ashley said. "Fish *cannot* sing."

"That's what you think," the boy said.

"We know what we heard," the mother added. "I'm going to call all our cousins! They just have to come hear those sharks."

The mother grabbed her little boy's hand, and the family hurried away.

"I wonder if those singing sharks have something to do with Mr. Kramer's problem at the shark exhibit," I said.

"Let's find out," Ashley said. She hung a CLOSED sign on our detective stand. We grabbed our backpacks and headed toward

Terrors of the Deep.

"Come on, Clue," I called. Clue hurried after Ashley and me.

Before we reached Terrors of the Deep, we ran into Mr. Kramer. He looked upset.

"Mr. Kramer, you won't believe the crazy story we just heard," I started to say.

Mr. Kramer groaned. "Don't tell me!" he said. "You heard that Sea World has singing sharks!"

"That's right," Ashley replied. "A nice family just told us all about them."

Mr. Kramer mopped beads of sweat off his forehead with a huge white handkerchief. "Mary-Kate and Ashley, you have to help me! If word gets out that the sharks are singing, Sea World will be ruined!"

"But why?" I asked. "That family *liked* listening to your sharks. They're going to tell all their cousins to come hear them."

"Right," Ashley said. "And you like visitors at Sea World. So what's the problem?"

"The problem is that sharks *can't* sing," Mr. Kramer answered. "People will make fun of us." He turned pale. "They might even say I was trying to fool everyone on purpose! Just to bring more visitors to the park!"

"No problem," Ashley said. "Just tell everyone that the sharks are *not* singing."

"I can't do that," Mr. Kramer said. He started mopping his forehead again. "Because they *are* singing! I heard them, too!" Mr. Kramer moaned. "I'd better see Dr. Charlene Finn right away!"

"Wait! Who's Dr. Charlene Finn?" I called.

"She's an ichthyologist!" Mr. Kramer replied, as he rushed off.

*Hmmmmm.*

"What should *we* do, Ashley?" I asked.

"We should get over to Terrors of the Deep," Ashley said. "Because Mr. Kramer is wrong. There *is* something fishy at Sea World. And it may be our next big mystery!"

# Chapter 2

"Here they are!" I called as we stepped into the underwater glass tunnel.

Through the glass, we watched the sharks swimming all around. They had long, pointy noses, and small, dark eyes, and rows of very sharp teeth.

"'Sharks can grow to be fifty feet long,'" I read a sign next to me. "'And they can swim very fast. More than thirty miles per hour.' Hey! That's as fast as a car on a street!"

One of the sharks swam close to the tunnel and opened its mouth really wide.

"Grrrrrr," Clue growled.

"Yikes!" Ashley yelped. She jumped away from the glass. "I don't know if these sharks can sing," she said. "But I'm sure of one

13

thing. They look mean."

"They aren't mean. And of course they can sing," a man behind us said.

"They can?" Ashley and I whirled around.

Behind us stood three men. They all wore colorful scarves wrapped around their heads. And they each held a long, thin fishing pole.

"I'm Captain Coleslaw," the man in the blue scarf said. "Ahoy, maties!"

Ashley and I stared at him.

"That's pirate talk for 'hello,'" Captain Coleslaw explained.

"Are you real pirates?" I asked. "I thought pirates were just in the movies!"

"Well, you thought wrong," the captain answered. "Meet my fellow buccaneers. That's another way to say 'pirates,'" he told me.

The captain pointed to a short, chubby man who was chewing a sandwich. "This is First Mate Murray," he said.

Murray's mouth was too full to talk, so he

nodded a hello.

"And this is Pirate Patches," Captain Coleslaw added.

A man wearing a black eye patch shook our hands. He also had on a set of head-phones and carried a small radio. He wore a red vest.

"Don't forget my parrot, Harvey," Patches said. He pointed to the green bird that perched on his shoulder. "Harvey doesn't talk much."

Ashley and I tried not to laugh. Of course Harvey didn't talk much. He wasn't a real parrot. He was a stuffed animal.

"Well, it's nice to meet you," Ashley said. "We've never met real pirates before."

"Not many folks have," Captain Coleslaw said.

"We spend most of our time traveling the world, doing pirate things," Patches said.

"You mean, you steal from sailors and set their ships on fire?" I asked.

Murray blushed. "Not really. Now we mostly look for places to buy a really good sandwich," he answered.

Captain Coleslaw frowned. "That's not true!" he said. "We are a brazen bunch of barnacles!"

"Don't mind the captain," Murray whispered to us. "He's just upset because we *stopped* being pirates. We don't work at all now," he added. "We live in the Senior Citizen Center."

"That sounds nice," I said.

"It's not bad," Murray said. "We take long walks on the beach. And we like to go fishing at Sea World."

"You mean, you like *pretending* to fish," Ashley said. "Fishing isn't allowed at Sea World."

"You're right," Patches said. He leaned his fishing pole against the glass. So did Murray and Captain Coleslaw.

Suddenly a voice came from the shark

tank! I listened in surprise.

"Welcome, ladies and gentlemen!" the voice called. "For our first number, we'd like to sing, 'I'm Waiting in the Rain Because You Are My Umbrella.'"

And then we heard music.

I grabbed Ashley's arm. "I don't believe it!" I exclaimed. "These sharks really *are* singing!"

# Chapter 3

"...That's why I'm waiting in the rain," the sharks sang out.

"They can sing country-and-western songs," Ashley exclaimed in surprise. "They're good!"

She dug into her backpack and pulled out our tape recorder. "We should tape these singing sharks," she told me. "It's our first clue."

"Right," I said. I reached for my detective notebook and started writing: MYSTERY: Sharks are singing, but everyone knows that sharks *can't* sing. EVIDENCE: We heard them.

The song came to an end.

"Thank you. Thank you for coming to Sea

World to hear us sing!" one of the sharks said.

"Hey, Mary-Kate, these aren't just singing sharks!" Ashley exclaimed. "They're singing and *talking* sharks!"

"And they always say 'thank you,'" Captain Coleslaw added. "Even sharks from the deep blue sea know it's important to be polite."

I wrote down that information in my notebook, too: CLUES: Sharks can also talk. And they are always polite.

"Well, girls, we have to go," Patches told us. "I think First Mate Murray needs another sandwich."

The pirates hurried away.

Ashley shook her head. "Poor Mr. Kramer. How will we prove that sharks can't sing when we just heard them singing?"

"I don't know, Ashley. Let's find more clues," I said.

We visited the whales and the penguins.

They didn't sing a note. Next we tried the turtles. Nothing. Not a single sound.

"I think we need help to figure out this mystery," I told Ashley.

"And I know just who can help us," Ashley said. "The same person that Mr. Kramer went to see—Dr. Charlene Finn, the ichthyologist!"

We called Clue to follow us. Then we hurried to Dr. Finn's office. She greeted us with a big smile.

"Nice to meet you," Dr. Finn said to Ashley and me. "Come in my office and make yourselves at home."

Ashley and I looked around Dr. Finn's office.

There were models of sharks on the floor and on her desk. There were photos of sharks hanging on the walls.

There were books about sharks crammed onto the shelves. And there was a real shark tooth sitting on her desk. It was big—and *very* sharp.

"This doesn't look like a doctor's office," I told her.

"That's because I'm not the kind of doctor you see when you're sick," Dr. Finn said. "I'm a scientist. I study everything there is to know about sharks."

"But I thought scientists looked like the ones on TV," Ashley said. "You know, short and bald with thick glasses."

Dr. Finn laughed. She was tall and pretty with short black hair, big brown eyes, and dark brown skin.

"How can I help you?" she asked.

"It's about the singing sharks. We—" Ashley began to say.

"Aren't sharks incredible?" Dr. Finn asked. "Did you know they are some of the best hunters in the sea?"

"Actually, we *didn't* know," I told her.

"And of course, you've seen how many teeth they have," she added. "Why, some sharks have *seven* rows of teeth!"

"That *is* incredible," Ashley said. "We can see why you like sharks so much. But—"

"*Like* sharks? No. Not me." Dr. Finn laughed out loud. "I *love* sharks! They are truly wonderful creatures."

"Yes, sharks are definitely awesome," I told her. "And you've told us some really interesting facts about them."

"But you haven't told us the one thing we really need to know," Ashley added. She took a deep breath. "Can they really talk and sing?" she asked.

"Of course not!" Dr. Finn laughed louder than before. "There is absolutely no way that sharks can talk *or* sing," she said.

"But we heard the sharks sing at Terrors of the Deep," I explained. "We even made a recording. Listen."

I dug out our tape recorder and played the tape of the sharks singing.

"They've got rhythm. And they can really

carry a tune," Dr. Finn said. "But those can't be sharks singing. It must be some kind of a trick. Of course, country and western is *not* my favorite kind of music, and I—"

"Thank you, Dr. Finn," Ashley said. "But we have to get going now. We need to help Mr. Kramer before he gets into trouble. We have to find some way to prove that *he* isn't making the sharks talk or sing."

"I see," Dr. Finn said. She reached up and grabbed a book from her shelf. "Take this. It's one of my favorite shark books," she told us. "It might make your job easier."

"Thanks, but we're not worried," I said. "We'll get to the bottom of this—and soon. Because the Trenchcoat Twins always solve the crime..."

"...by dinner time," Ashley finished.

"That reminds me." I glanced at my watch. "Yikes! It's almost noon!" I said. "We promised to meet Mom and Dad for lunch in exactly three minutes!"

Ashley and I grabbed our backpacks. Clue slowly got to her feet.

"Hurry, Clue," I told her. "We can't stop for *anything*."

Ashley, Clue, and I raced back toward the middle of Sea World.

"Wait, Mary-Kate!" Ashley called. "We have to stop for this!" Ashley pointed straight ahead.

I saw a tall, thin man whose face was red with anger. His fists were raised in the air, and he looked as if he was going to hit the person who stood in front of him—a pudgy, worried-looking person with a mustache.

"Mr. Kramer!" I yelled. "Look out!"

# Chapter 4

We rushed to Mr. Kramer's side.

"What are you doing?" I shouted at the angry man.

"Woof!" Clue barked.

"Leave Mr. Kramer alone," Ashley added.

"Why should I?" the man asked. "He says there are no singing sharks at Sea World. My family drove a long way to hear those sharks sing!" The man glared at Mr. Kramer.

"I'm sorry, sir," Mr. Kramer said. "I know what people are saying. But sharks really *can't* sing. I can't sell tickets to something that's phony."

"Then I want my money back," the man said.

Mr. Kramer sighed. He pulled a piece of

paper from his pocket and wrote a note on it. "Take this to the front gate. They'll give you back your money," he said.

The man gathered his family together and they stormed away. Mr. Kramer groaned. "Did you hear that?" he asked.

"That man was so loud, everybody in Sea World heard him!" I answered.

"People really want to see the singing sharks," Mr. Kramer told us. "When I give them back their money, they get mad."

"The singing is some kind of a trick," I told him. I explained our visit with Dr. Finn.

"Well, I hope you figure out how to stop it," Mr. Kramer said. "I'm going to Dr. Finn's office again. Call if you need me."

"No problem," I said. "We're on the case!"

"Or we will be, as soon as we meet Mom and Dad for lunch," Ashley pointed out.

"Oh, I saw your family in the refreshment area next to the dolphin show," Mr. Kramer said. "Look for them at the table closest to the three new flagpoles."

We thanked Mr. Kramer and called Clue. We all hurried across the park. "There are the flagpoles," I told Ashley.

Up ahead, we saw three metal flagpoles. One flew an American flag. Another flew the Sea World flag. And the third flew a flag with a big dolphin on it.

"And there are Mom and Dad," Ashley said. Our parents had on the bathing suits they wore when they worked with the dolphins.

I groaned. "And Trent and Lizzie are with them," I said.

Trent is our big brother. He's eleven. And he is very excited about being at Sea World, in Florida. Trent has a big lizard collection, and Florida is famous for its lizards.

We think *Trent* is famous—for being a real pain. He's always teasing us and saying that we're not *real* detectives.

Our little sister, Lizzie, is six. She thinks

we're *great* detectives. So great that she always wants to tag along with us.

Clue began to whine.

"It's okay, girl," I told her. "I know you're thirsty after all that running around."

Clue followed Ashley and me to our picnic table. We gave her some water.

"It's about time you got here," Trent said. "Mom wouldn't let us eat without you guys, and I'm starving."

"Me too," Lizzie said.

Ashley and I sat down. Mom and Dad handed out hamburgers, French fries, and drinks.

"You guys are in big trouble for being so late," Trent told us.

"Fifteen minutes late, to be exact," Dad said.

"Guilty," I replied, shaking ketchup onto my French fries.

"But with an explanation," Ashley added. She gulped down her drink. "We were trying to help Mr. Kramer solve the mystery of the singing sharks."

Trent laughed. "We heard all about that. And there is no mystery. Because sharks *can't* sing. Right, Dad?" he asked.

"Right," Dad said, taking a bite of his hamburger.

"That's what we thought," I said. "But we heard them sing—and talk, too."

"Well, I don't know how," Mom said. "We know dolphins can understand certain signals. Like the signals they hear through our computer program. And they can make different sounds."

"But dolphins don't sing or speak the way we do," Dad added. "And neither do sharks."

"See?" Trent said to Ashley and me. "You wasted your morning. You don't have a big important case at all."

"Okay, big shot," I replied. "What important things did *you* do today?"

"I collected a zillion lizards!" Trent said.

He reached below the table and held up his lizard cage. It was stuffed with lizards of every size. He opened the cage door and took out a long, green, scaly one.

"How do you like this one?" he asked.

"Which one of you is the lizard?" Ashley asked.

"Ha ha ha!" Trent said.

Clue tried to bat the lizard with her paw. She loves playing with other animals.

"No, Clue!" Trent said. He quickly put the lizard back in its cage.

"That's enough from all of you," Mom told us. "Finish eating. It's time for Dad and me to get back to work."

"Yes," Dad added. "Trent, please take Lizzie back to our hotel room for her nap. The shuttle bus stop is right here."

"Why can't Mary-Kate and Ashley do it?" Trent asked. He *hates* to take care of Lizzie.

"Because it's your turn now and their turn later," Mom said.

"And Trent, take Clue with you," Dad added. "She looks really hot and tired. She could use a rest."

Trent, Lizzie, and Clue headed toward the shuttle bus stop.

"We should get back on our case," I told Ashley. I jumped up to get ready to go.

"Not so fast," Mom told me. "Dad and I also have a job for you and Ashley to do."

"What kind of job?" I asked.

Dad grinned. "Don't worry, we think you'll like it," he said. "We need you to help with *our* mystery!"

# Chapter 5

"You have a mystery?" I asked in surprise.

"Yes. Come with us. I'll explain the whole thing," Dad said.

Ashley and I followed Mom and Dad over to the dolphins. The dolphins were swimming together along the edge of the pool. Mom knelt down and one of the dolphins swam over to her. Mom rubbed the dolphin's head.

"Don't worry," she told him. "Mary-Kate and Ashley are here to help us. You won't be confused much longer," she said.

"I hope we can help," I told Mom.

"Well, you remember how our dolphin-communication program works, don't you?" Mom asked us.

"Sure. The computer sends signals under-water to the dolphins," I said.

"That's how they know when to do their natural moves—like leaping out of the water or twirling in the air. The dolphins hear the signal, and then do a move," Ashley added.

"Usually," Mom said. "But somehow, the signals from our computer are getting mixed up with signals from someplace else. The dolphins can't tell which sounds to listen to."

"We can't find out where the other signals are coming from, so we don't know how to stop them," Dad added.

"I'm not sure how to figure that out," I said. "Do you have any ideas, Ashley?"

"No." Ashley shrugged. "But I know what we should do. Research!"

Ashley opened up her detective manual. "Here it is—sound signals and sound waves." She read out loud:

"'Sound waves travel through air or through liquids or through solids. They travel more slowly in liquids than in solids.'"

"What does that mean?" I asked her.

"I don't know yet," Ashley said. She read some more. "'Some types of sound waves can carry information in signals. Radio waves, for example. Antennas pick up the signals of radio waves and turn them into sounds that we can hear when we turn on our radios.'"

"Some other sound waves are confusing the dolphins. Right?" I asked Mom and Dad.

"Right," Dad said. "We'll show you."

Dad typed some information into the computer that was set up next to the pool. Mom dove into the pool and listened to the signals through a pair of headphones.

The dolphins heard the signals, too. One dolphin leaped out of the water. Another one leaped and twirled around. The two dolphins almost bumped into each other.

"Stop!" Mom called. She waved at Dad to stop typing and climbed out of the pool. She looked really upset.

"It happened again," she said. "I heard all kinds of other signals in the water."

Dad shook his head. "I don't get it. There were no other signals last year, when we set up the program."

Dad scratched his head, looking puzzled. "Maybe you can think of some way to help," he said to us.

"Well, you should always be logical," Ashley told him. "So, first you should figure out what's different now from last year."

"And use our research," I added. "Like the fact that sound waves can travel through air or liquids or solids."

"We already know that the signals are traveling through a liquid—through the water in the dolphin pool," Dad said.

Ashley looked thoughtful. She gazed all around the pool. "I'm just wondering.... metal is a solid, isn't it?" she asked.

"Of course." Dad frowned.

Ashley jabbed me in the side. She pointed behind the dolphin pool. I stared where she was pointing.

*Hmmmmm.*

"Ashley—are you thinking what I'm thinking?" I asked.

"What are you thinking?" Mom asked.

"The flagpoles!" Ashley and I said at once.

Our parents stared at us in disbelief.

"The flagpoles are new," I explained. "They weren't here last year when you set up the dolphin-communication program."

"And they're made of metal," Ashley added.

"And metal can carry sound waves!" Mom finished.

"Of course!" Dad smacked himself on the forehead. "I should have seen it myself," he said. "Those new metal flagpoles are working like radio antennas. They're attracting radio signals from all around and sending them into the water."

"So the dolphins are hearing our computer signals and the radio signals carried in the flagpoles," Mom said. "No wonder they're so confused!"

"I'll ask Mr. Kramer to move the flagpoles," Dad said.

Mom gave Ashley and me a big hug. "Thank you so much," she said.

A crackling noise suddenly blared from a loudspeaker overhead.

"Ladies and gentlemen," a man's voice announced. "This is Wild Willy Wayne, the disc jockey at WXYR, Orlando's hottest radio station! We're getting ready to bring you a very special radio show. A show starring some amazing singing sharks! They're coming to you live—from Terrors of the Deep at Sea World!"

"Oh, no!" I said. "Ashley—somebody has to stop that show!"

# Chapter 6

Ashley and I raced back to Terrors of the Deep. Wild Willy Wayne sat behind a microphone in a radio-broadcast booth. The booth had been set up beside the shark exhibit. A crowd of people was already gathering.

Captain Coleslaw, Pirate Patches, and First Mate Murray stood in front of Wild Willy.

"So, what do you say? Will you let us perform with the singing sharks?" Captain Coleslaw asked him.

"I told you, I'm not sure yet," Wild Willy answered.

"Of course, the sharks are the stars of the show," Captain Coleslaw said. "But we're pretty good singers, too."

"Sure. I can sing any song, as long as the

words are written down," Patches said.

"And we tell the best pirate jokes in the business," Murray added.

"Besides, the sharks only sing for us," Patches said.

"Well, I have to hear them sing now," Wild Willy said. "Before we go ahead with the live broadcast of their show."

"Naturally!" the captain replied. "Come with me, matey."

Captain Coleslaw and the others led Wild Willy up to the front of the shark exhibit. We went with them.

The pirates leaned their fishing poles against the glass. The sharks swam close by.

"Ladies and gentlemen!" one of the sharks said. "Introducing the amazing, sensational, singing sharks of Sea World!"

The sharks started singing.

"Wait a minute," I said. "I have a hunch that this song is playing on the radio right now!"

The song finished, and the shark said, "Thank you! Thank you for coming to Sea World to hear us sing!"

The crowd clapped and cheered and whistled. Captain Coleslaw turned to Wild Willy. "The crowd loved them! Now what do you say?" the captain asked.

"I say, your sharks are terrific!" Wild Willy shook Captain Coleslaw's hand. "You have a job! Call my boss at the radio station. Tell him you're going to sing with the sharks."

The pirates each grabbed a telephone.

"Not so fast," I called to them. "Those sharks will never sing on the radio," I said.

The pirates gasped in horror.

Wild Willy Wayne looked puzzled. "Why not?" he asked.

"Because those sharks *can't* sing!" I announced.

"Never have, never will," Ashley added. "And we know how to prove it!"

Ashley and I think Sea World is the greatest—
especially when there's a mystery to solve! And we
*love* to solve mysteries.

The minute we reached our detective stand at Sea
World, we found a mystery—singing sharks!
Sharks can't sing, can they?

We rushed to the shark exhibit, Terrors of the Deep, to look for clues. There we met Captain Coleslaw, Pirate Patches, and First Mate Murray. They were real-life pirates!

Suddenly, a voice came from behind the glass. "Welcome, Ladies and Gentlemen," it said. Then we heard singing! Wow—these sharks really *could* sing!

"We should tape these singing sharks," Ashley said.
"It's our first clue."

Next, we visited the whales and some other
animals to see if *they* could sing too. Not a note!

We went to see Dr. Finn, the shark expert. She told us sharks definitely *cannot* sing. Dr. Finn said someone must be playing a trick on Sea World. But who? And how?

We sped back to the shark exhibit. We had a lot of work to do if we wanted to solve *this* crime by dinner time!

The sharks were singing a different song this time. "Wait a minute," Ashley said to me. "Are you sure these sharks are singing? Because this song is playing on the radio right now!"

Captain Coleslaw was talking loudly to the other pirates. "These sharks are going to be major stars," he said, "with a little help from us, of course!" W wondered what *that* meant.

Something smelled fishy—so we followed the pirates outside. They were on the phone, trying to set up a concert starring the singing sharks—and themselves!

We had to think—and fast! If the song was on the [...] ow could it be coming from the shark [...] And what did the pirates have to do with [...] died all our evidence again, especially our [...] rding.

We were stumped. Until we figured out that the music came from the radio—not from the sharks! The sneaky pirates used their metal fishing poles as antennas to pick up sound signals from the radio station.

"The signals travel up the poles and into the glass," Ashley explained. "The glass acts like a radio speaker. It makes the music loud enough for everyone to hear." Case solved?

Not so fast! The sharks weren't just singing. They also knew how to *talk*! We figured out how they did that too! Can you?

# Chapter 7

Wild Willy Wayne stared at me. "If the sharks weren't singing, where did that song come from?" he asked.

"From your radio station!" I told him.

Wild Willy laughed out loud. "But I wasn't broadcasting my live show on the radio yet," he said.

"But WXYR *was* broadcasting," I told him. "The radio station isn't far away from here. Not far at all for three metal antennas to pick up the radio signals."

"What metal antennas?" Captain Coleslaw asked. "There are no antennas here at Sea World."

"Oh, yes, there are," I said. "Fishing-pole antennas!"

"Why, that's...that's ridiculous!" Pirate Patches sputtered.

"Unbelievable," Captain Coleslaw added.

I smiled. "Then you won't mind if we borrow your fishing poles for a minute, will you?" I asked the captain.

Captain Coleslaw swallowed hard. "Of course we don't mind," he replied.

Captain Coleslaw handed me his fishing pole. Pirate Patches handed his pole to Ashley. And First Mate Murray handed his pole to Wild Willy.

"Lean your poles against the glass!" I said.

Ashley, Wild Willy, and I leaned the poles against the glass. We heard music.

"Hey. It worked!" Wild Willy said.

"The fishing poles are acting like radio antennas," I explained. "They're picking up sound signals from WXYR. The radio station is really close to Sea World."

"The signals travel up the poles and into the glass," Ashley added. "The glass acts like a radio speaker. It makes the music loud enough for everyone to hear."

"So we were really listening to the radio—not to singing sharks," I added. "We figured it out because we knew that the flagpoles by the dolphin show acted as antennas, too."

Wild Willy's face turned red with anger. He turned to the pirates. "You tricked me! You tricked *everyone!*" he shouted. "The singing sharks are fakes!"

Captain Coleslaw glared at Ashley and me. Pirate Patches seemed really upset. First Mate Murray seemed confused.

"Sorry, pirates," I told them. "But Olsen and Olsen did it again. We solved the mystery of the singing sharks."

I raised my hand to slap Ashley a high five. But Captain Coleslaw stopped me.

"Not so fast, super sleuths!" he said. "You two haven't solved a thing!"

"We haven't?" Ashley and I said at the same time.

"They haven't?" Wild Willy repeated.

"No, they haven't," Captain Coleslaw said. "I admit it—the sharks *can't* sing. We did use the fishing poles as radio antennas."

Pirate Patches shrugged. "No harm meant. Just a bit of pirate fun," he said.

"Right. But the sharks *still* do something very special," Captain Coleslaw added. "They talk."

Ashley frowned. "He's right," she said. "The sharks introduced the songs. And they said 'thank you' to the crowd here at Sea World. That *didn't* come from the radio."

"So you can still do a live broadcast with

*talking* sharks," Captain Coleslaw told Wild Willy. "Talking sharks are very cool!"

Wild Willy checked his watch. "We're supposed to go on the air in one hour. I'd better call the station and ask them what to do."

Wild Willy hurried toward the nearest pay phone. The three pirates hurried after him. Patches was waving his arms around. I saw a piece of paper fly out of his vest pocket. It landed on the ground.

I bent over and picked it up. The paper was covered with numbers. "Ashley, look at this," I said.

"It's just a bunch of numbers," Ashley said. She read it out loud:

19,11,23    10,13,3,24    23,13,5
4,5,26,24    24,11,26,12    16,17,12,1
14,13    15,13,8    17    12,19,26,22
12,24,17,23    17,19,17,23    15,8,13,22
24,11,1    12,11,17,8,21,12

Ashley shrugged. "This doesn't make any sense. We'll give it back to Patches later," she told me.

I tucked the paper into my backpack.

"Right now, we should get back to our detective stand," Ashley went on. "We need to go over this case. Because Olsen and Olsen *didn't* solve the whole mystery," she said. "We're stumped!"

"You're right," I said. "And we only have one hour to figure out how those sharks were talking!"

There was no one near our detective stand. We sat down and Ashley pulled out our tape recorder.

"Let's be calm and logical," Ashley said. "First, we should listen to our tape again."

Ashley pushed the play button. We heard the sharks introduce their song. We heard the song from the radio. When it was over, we heard the crowd applaud.

Then we heard one of the sharks say,

"Thank you! Thank you for coming to Sea World to hear us sing!"

I pushed the stop button. "I'm still stumped," I said.

"We have to try harder," Ashley told me.

Ashley reached into her backpack for Dr. Finn's book. She opened it and began reading. "Wow! They're really in trouble," she said.

"You mean, *we're* in trouble, don't you?" I asked.

Ashley shook her head. "No. The *sharks* are in trouble."

"How can that be?" I asked.

"The book says that sharks are in danger from people because people dump garbage in the ocean. The sharks eat the garbage, and sometimes it kills them."

"That's terrible!" I said.

"Sharks have been found dead with cans, and shoes, and even license plates in their stomachs," Ashley told me.

"That's interesting *and* important," I said. "But it doesn't help solve our new mystery."

Ashley turned a few more pages. "Here's a picture of the inside of a shark," she said.

She showed me a picture of a shark's heart, brain, and stomach. "Sharks are a lot like humans inside," she said.

She stared more closely at the picture. "Hey, look," she said. "Sharks don't have vocal cords!"

"Let me see that," I said. I took the book from her.

"But you need vocal cords to speak," I said. "We learned that in school."

"I know," Ashley said. "So if sharks don't have any vocal cords—" she began.

"They can't talk!" I finished. "Which puts us right back where we started." I sighed. "Nowhere!"

"Why don't you quit this case? Go for a swim!" a man's voice called out angrily from behind us.

Ashley and I jumped up and spun around. There was nothing behind us. Only a bunch of bushes and flowers.

"Who said that?" I called into the bushes.

"None of your business!" the voice answered. "Stay away from the sharks!"

I stared at the bushes and flowers. "Ashley," I whispered. "There's nobody there!"

"Somebody has to be there!" Ashley said. "Bushes don't talk!"

We stared at the bushes. They moved—and something jumped out at us!

# Chapter 9

"*Eeeaaahh!*" I screamed.

"*Eeeaaahh!*" Ashley screamed.

A squirrel ran out of the bushes and raced past our detective stand.

"Oh. It was only a squirrel," I said. My voice was shaking.

"Well, *somebody* was there," Ashley replied. "That voice didn't come out of thin air! Or from the squirrel!"

"You're right," I said. "We should check out the bushes for clues."

Ashley marched into the bushes. She dropped to her knees and started pulling branches aside. "Come on, Mary-Kate," she called. "Help me."

A few minutes later, Ashley and I were tired and sweaty and covered with scratches. But we hadn't found one single clue. Ashley looked disgusted. "We'll never solve this case," she said. "We need to come up with some clues, and fast!"

I snapped my fingers.

"We need someone with a nose for clues! Follow me." I raced toward the shuttle bus stop. Ashley ran to catch up to me.

"Where are we going?" she asked.

"Back to the hotel," I told her. "To get Clue!"

The shuttle bus took us back to our hotel. We raced up to our hotel room.

Clue was taking a snooze in the middle of the living-room floor.

"Wake up, sleepyhead," I called into one of her long, floppy ears. "You have a mystery to solve."

Clue pulled herself up and slowly wagged her tail. "Woof!" she barked, and licked my hand. I patted her head.

Lizzie was sitting nearby, watching a puppet show on TV. A dragon, an alligator, and a man were telling jokes to each other.

"Shhh!" Lizzie called to us. "I can't hear this show!"

"Where's Trent?" I asked her.

"In his room, playing with all his new lizards," Lizzie answered. "I wish he'd let *me* play with them," she added.

Clue went over to the TV and lay down again.

"You don't have time for TV now, Clue," I told her.

"I think Clue wants to hear what the dragon says next," Lizzie told me. "He's funny."

I rolled my eyes. "That dragon isn't real!" I said. "He's only a puppet."

"He is too real!" Lizzie said. "He can talk."

"The puppet isn't talking. The *man* is talking for the puppet," I explained.

"The man is *not* talking," Lizzie said. "He's

not moving his lips or anything."

"That's because he's a ventriloquist," I told her. "That means he can talk without moving his lips."

"You're crazy," Lizzie told us. "Now the alligator is talking, and he's nowhere near the man!"

I sighed. "Lizzie, I don't have time to argue. We have to get back to work."

I pulled Clue's collar. "Let's go," I said.

"Not so fast," a voice called.

Trent!

He appeared in the doorway to his room. He was holding one of his lizards. More lizards crawled over the floor behind him.

"You can't go anywhere," Trent said. "It's your turn to take care of Lizzie."

"Not now," Ashley told him. "Mom and Dad said our turn would be later."

"Well, it *is* later," Trent said.

"Yes, but we have to track down some really important evidence," I said.

"That's too bad," Trent replied. "It's my turn to have fun. So, good-bye."

Trent waved good-bye, holding a lizard in one hand.

"Arf!" Clue barked. She ran toward the lizard. It jumped out of Trent's hand, and Clue started chasing it.

All the lizards in Trent's room tried to get away from Clue. Some disappeared under the bed and under the dresser. Others headed for the closet.

"Wait! Stop! Come back!" Trent yelled. He chased after the lizards.

"Lizzie, you better help Trent catch those lizards," Ashley called.

I grabbed Clue and snapped on her leash. "Good luck, Trent! See you later," I called.

Ashley, Clue, and I ran out the door and back to the shuttle bus.

*Yes!*

Olsen and Olsen and Clue were back on the case!

# Chapter 10

"Okay, silent partner. Do your stuff," I told Clue. "Help us find some really important evidence."

Clue sniffed at our detective stand. She sniffed at the air. She sniffed through the bushes where we saw the squirrel. Suddenly she ran across the path and began to sniff at the bushes there.

"No, Clue," I told her. "The voice we heard came from *behind* our stand. You won't find any evidence over there."

Clue still pawed at the bushes.

"I think she found something," Ashley said.

We hurried across the path. We saw some long red threads tangled around the leaves.

"Nothing here but some threads," I said.

"Remember what Great-grandma Olive said," Ashley told me. "Pay attention to *everything*."

Ashley took out her magnifying glass and examined the threads. "Hmmm. Red threads. That seems familiar for some reason," she said.

"Well, Pirate Patches always wears a red vest," I said. "And that reminds me! We never gave him back the note that we found!"

I pulled the piece of paper out of my backpack and handed it to Ashley. She lifted her magnifying glass and began to examine the piece of paper.

"What are you doing that for?" I asked.

"To see if this paper has red threads on it. Aha!" she exclaimed.

Ashley handed me the magnifying glass. I peered through it. I saw tiny specks of red thread on the paper.

"The threads are the same," Ashley said.

"That means Patches was in these bushes. I think he's the one who told us to stay away from the sharks."

"But the person who warned us was standing *behind* the bushes," I said.

"Was he?" Ashley asked. "I mean, we didn't *see* him standing there."

"No. But we heard him there," I said.

"We *thought* we heard him there," Ashley told me. "Just like we *thought* we heard the sharks sing."

*Hmmmmm.*

"You think the voice behind us was some kind of a trick," I said. I stared at the piece of paper in my hand. I pulled my detective manual out of my backpack. I flipped to the section on codes and pulled out my Super-Duper Snooper Decoder.

"If these numbers are a secret code, this decoder will turn the numbers into letters," I said.

The decoder was easy to use. Each number stood for a letter. When I wrote down the letters, they spelled out words.

"Hey, this is fun," I told Ashley. "See, the number 12 stands for the letter *S*. The number 19 stands for *W*."

"But what does it spell?" Ashley asked.

"You're never going to believe it," I said when I finished. I showed her the message I had written down.

"Mary-Kate, it's time to call Mr. Kramer!" Ashley exclaimed.

We raced over to the pay phone. I dialed Mr. Kramer's office number.

"Mr. Kramer, your worries are over," I said. "We solved the mystery! Call Dr. Finn and meet us at the WXYR broadcast booth in five minutes."

Ashley, Clue, and I raced over to the booth. Captain Coleslaw, Pirate Patches, and First Mate Murray were already there.

"Hold the broadcast!" Ashley shouted. "Those sharks *won't* be talking today!"

# Chapter 11

Everyone at the broadcast booth turned to stare at us.

"Of course the sharks will talk!" Captain Coleslaw shouted. Patches and Murray both nodded.

"Why won't they talk?" Wild Willy asked.

"Sharks *can't* talk," Dr. Finn said.

"Will somebody tell me what's going on?" Mr. Kramer asked.

We quickly told Mr. Kramer how the pirates had used their fishing poles to send radio signals into the shark exhibit.

"They made it seem as if the sharks could sing," I said.

"But Dr. Finn is right. Sharks can't sing or talk," Ashley added. "It's impossible! Because they don't have vocal cords."

"They don't?" Wild Willy asked.

Captain Coleslaw raised his eyebrows. "Well, shiver me timbers!"

"I can't believe it," Murray told us.

"Believe it," I said. "Sharks can't talk. But pirates can. Especially pirates who know how to throw their voices."

"Now what are you talking about?" Mr. Kramer asked.

"Our little sister, Lizzie, was watching a puppet show on TV," I explained. "The man working the puppets was a good ventriloquist. He made it seem as if the puppets were talking, even when he wasn't next to them. That's because he could throw his voice."

"Huh? Like a baseball?" Wild Willy asked.

"No. Throwing your voice means you make it sound as if your voice is coming from somewhere else," Ashley said.

Captain Coleslaw was insulted. "I don't

know how to throw my voice," he said.

"You don't," I agreed. "But Pirate Patches does."

Patches' face turned bright red. "How did you figure it out?" he asked.

I explained how we found the note that fell from Patches' pocket. And that we found red threads on the note and on the bushes in front of our detective stand.

"Then we remembered that Patches told Wild Willy that he could sing any song, as long as the words were written down," I added.

"That proved Patches doesn't have a very good memory," Ashley said. "If he wanted to scare us away from this case, he would have to write down the exact words to say."

I showed Mr. Kramer the note we found and the decoder. "When we cracked this code, the message spelled these words." I took a deep breath and imitated Patches' voice: "Why don't you quit this case? Go for a swim! Stay away from the sharks!" I said.

"Not a bad imitation," Patches told me.

"Thanks," I said.

"Wait," Mr. Kramer said. "How did Patches remember the warning without his note?"

"Oh, I had another copy in my other vest pocket," Patches said. "I make two copies of every note. I lose things a lot."

"This is all very interesting," Dr. Finn said. "I see how the pirates fooled people into thinking the sharks could sing. And I see that Patches tried to scare you off the case. But I'm still puzzled about one thing. How did the pirates know which songs were playing on the radio? Didn't the sharks announce their songs before they sang them?"

I grinned. "The answer is in Patches' headphones. Patches was listening to WXYR on his radio. And disc jockeys always announce a song before they play it," I said.

"So Patches heard what song was about to be played, and then he announced it by throwing his voice," Ashley added. "So it sounded as if the sharks introduced the songs."

"I'm completely amazed," Mr. Kramer said. "You pirates are certainly very clever."

"Thank you, sir," the captain told him.

"But you're not nearly as clever as Mary-Kate and Ashley. They figured it all out," Mr. Kramer added.

"We just put all the clues together," I said.

"You're really a good ventriloquist," Ashley told Patches. "You had us all fooled."

Captain Coleslaw sighed. "But the jig is still up, mates," he said to Pirate Patches and First Mate Murray.

Then he turned to Dr. Finn and Mr. Kramer. "I'm sorry, folks. We didn't mean any harm."

"It's true," Patches added. "We were just looking for a way to get back into show business."

"But I thought you were pirates," I said.

Captain Coleslaw blushed. "Aye, we *acted* the part of pirates," he said.

"We did a pirate show for years and years," Patches told us. "Then the folks who ran the show said we were too old to work. So we stopped acting, singing, and telling pirate jokes."

"You have no idea how bored we are," Murray added.

"We really miss performing," Patches said. "But I guess we'll never find a new job." He sighed.

Mr. Kramer grinned. "Don't be so sure about that," he said. "I'm so glad this mystery is cleared up that I'll help you out. I'll get you another job. And you'll sail the seven seas—like real pirates!"

"How will you ever do that?" Captain Coleslaw asked.

I groaned. "Oh, no," I said. "Not *another* mystery!"

# Chapter 12

The pirates were happy. Mr. Kramer was happy. Even Dr. Finn was happy. But Trent was *un*happy that we left him with Lizzie in the hotel room. Ashley and I were in *big* trouble.

We all went to the dolphin pool to find Mom and Dad. Ashley and I promised that we would take *two* turns baby-sitting for Lizzie the next day. That made Trent happy.

And Mr. Kramer told Mom and Dad how we solved the case of the singing sharks.

"You girls did a great job," Mom said.

"But we haven't solved *all* the mysteries," Ashley said. "We still don't know how Mr. Kramer will get the pirates a job in show business *and* let them sail the seven seas."

Mr. Kramer smiled. "That's my secret," he told us. "Right now, it's time for you to stop working and enjoy Sea World!"

Ashley and I gave each other a high five. We were definitely ready for some serious fun!

A week later, we were in our office in the attic of our house. The phone rang. Ashley and I answered the way we always do.

"Olsen and Olsen Mystery Agency," we said together.

"Will solve any crime—" I began.

"By dinner time," Ashley finished.

"Ahoy, maties!" a voice called. "It's Captain Coleslaw, with Pirate Patches and First Mate Murray."

"Ahoy, maties!" I said.

"What are you up to?" Ashley asked.

"We're sailing the seven seas!" First Mate Murray said.

"And we're back in show business!" Pirate

Patches added.

Captain Coleslaw explained. "Mr. Kramer got us a job on a cruise ship. We perform the dinner show. We sing songs, tell jokes—"

"And I do a great ventriloquist act with my trusty parrot, Harvey," Patches put in.

"But best of all, we get all the free food we can eat!" First Mate Murray exclaimed.

"Our ship will be in California on Saturday. We want you and your family to be our guests for the show," the captain said.

"We wouldn't miss it!" we replied.

On Saturday, our whole family got all dressed up. We couldn't wait to see the captain, Patches, and Murray again!

Their show was terrific. We laughed at Murray's jokes. And we clapped like crazy when the captain danced a pirate jig.

Then Patches made Harvey the parrot talk—and he even threw Harvey's voice!

It was really late when we got home. Mom and Dad ordered us straight to bed.

But Ashley and I were too excited to sleep.

"You know, Mary-Kate, I really miss Sea World," Ashley whispered. "There are such great mysteries there."

"I know what you mean, Ashley," I whispered back. "But there are mysteries waiting everywhere. And I have a hunch we'll find another mystery soon!"

\* \* \*

We have a special mystery for you to solve right now!

After the show, Murray the pirate told a great joke. But he told it to us in code. We figured it out. And now you can too!

Just turn to page 78 to make your own Super-Duper Snooper Decoder. Then use it to decode Pirate Murray's joke!

19 11 17 24   21 26 3 10   13 15   15 26 12 11
13 3 25 23   16 13 22 1 12   13 5 24   17 24
3 26 14 11 24?

17   12 24 17 8   15 26 12 11 *   **\* Answer:**
A star fish!

76

*Hi — from both of us!*

Aren't you glad we proved that sharks can't sing? We sure are! Cracking the secret code helped us crack the case. Now Ashley and I are headed for another hot mystery. And you can figure out where it takes place! Just use your Super-Duper Snooper Decoder on the next page to solve the riddle below:

17 24    13 5 8    11 13 24 1 25

19 1    10 13    24 11 1    11 5 25 17

19 11 1 9 1    17 9 1    19 1?

Our next case takes place in __ __ __ __ __ __.

(Find the decoded riddle and the answer at the bottom of this page)

Ashley and I had to stop a thief who was robbing the guests in our fancy hotel. How did we do it? Read all about it in *The Case Of The Hotel Who-Done-It*. In the meantime, if you have any questions, you can write us at:

MARY-KATE + ASHLEY'S FUN CLUB
859 HOLLYWOOD WAY, SUITE 412
BURBANK, CA 91505

We would love to hear from you!

*Love*
*Mary-Kate and Ashley*

# SUPER-DUPER SNOOPER DECODER

**Here's what you need to make your very own
Super-Duper Snooper Decoder—
just like Mary-Kate & Ashley's.**

**What you need:**
scissors
1 paper fastener

**1** Use scissors to cut out Circle 1 on page 79 and Circle 2 on page 81. Have an adult help you.

**2.** On Circle 1, cut out the two notches along the dotted lines.

**3.** Place Circle 1 on **top** of Circle 2.

**4.** Punch your paper fastener through the two circles at the dot in the middle of Circle 1 and all the way through the dot on Circle 2. Push back the two ends of the paper fastener to secure it in place. This will hold the two circles together.

**5.** Now you are ready to decode secret messages. All you have to do is turn the top circle on your Super-Duper Snooper Decoder. Let's try to decode this!

Message:   24 18 26 25 4

Turn the top circle to find 24 in one notched window. You will see the letter T appear in the other window. Write T on a piece of paper. Next turn the circle to find 18. 18 lines up with the letter W. Write W after T. Do the same with 26, 25, and 4. You should get the word TWINS.

**6.** Now you can decode the secret messages on pages 76 and 77!

**7.** You can also use your Super-Duper Snooper Decoder to send secret messages to your friends.

# CIRCLE 1

**SUPER-DUPER SNOOPER DECODER**

*The Adventures of*
**MARY-KATE & ASHLEY**

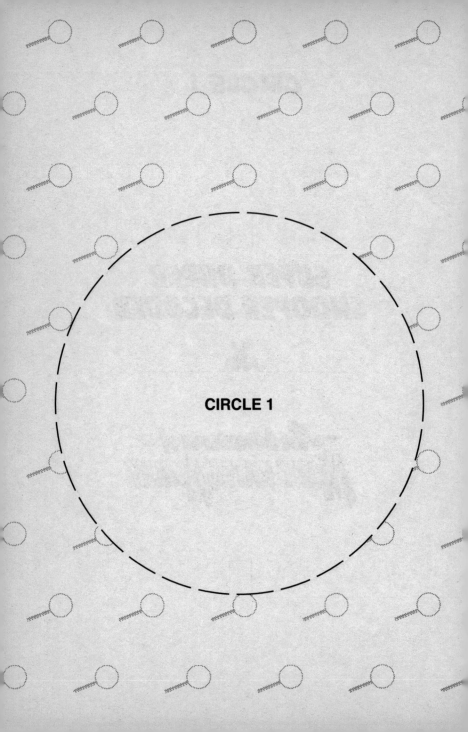

CIRCLE 1

# CIRCLE 2

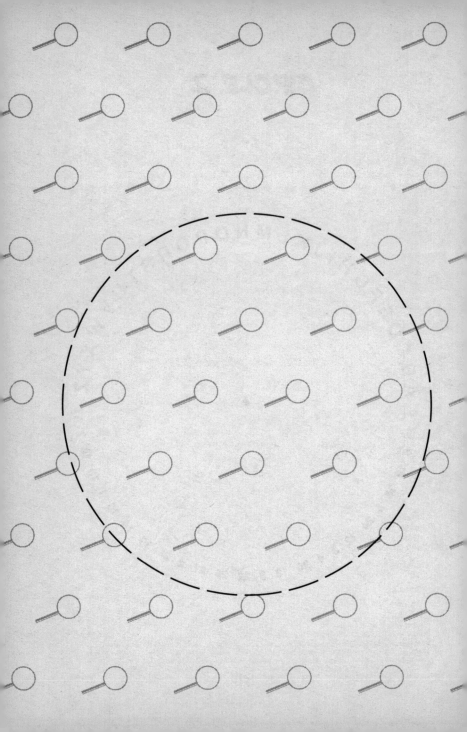

## The Adventures of
# MARY-KATE & ASHLEY™

### Look for the best-selling detective home video episodes.

| | |
|---|---|
| The Case Of The Volcano Adventure™ | Spring 97 Release |
| The Case Of The U.S. Navy Mystery™ | Spring 97 Release |
| The Case Of The Hotel Who•Done•It™ *NEW* | 53328-3 |
| The Case Of The Shark Encounter™ | 53320-3 |
| The Case Of The U.S. Space Camp® Mission™ | 53321-3 |
| The Case Of The Fun House Mystery™ | 53306-3 |
| The Case Of The Christmas Caper™ | 53305-3 |
| The Case Of The Sea World® Adventure™ | 53301-3 |
| The Case Of The Mystery Cruise™ | 53302-3 |
| The Case Of The Logical i Ranch™ | 53303-3 |
| The Case Of Thorn Mansion™ | 53300-3 |

# YOU'RE INVITED TO MARY-KATE & ASHLEY'S™

### Join the fun!

| | |
|---|---|
| You're Invited To Mary-Kate & Ashley's™ Sleepover Party™ | 53307-3 |
| You're Invited To Mary-Kate & Ashley's™ Hawaiian Beach Party™ *NEW* | 53329-3 |

### And also available:

| | |
|---|---|
| Mary-Kate and Ashley Olsen: Our First Video™ | 53304- |

**DUALSTAR VIDEO**

# The Adventures of
# MARY-KATE & ASHLEY™

# HOLLYWOOD
# SWEEPSTAKES

## YOU CAN WIN A TRIP
## TO HOLLYWOOD
## TO MEET MARY-KATE & ASHLEY!

**Complete this entry form and send to:**
The Adventures of Mary-Kate & Ashley™ Hollywood Sweepstakes
c/o Scholastic Trade Marketing Dept.
P.O. Box 7500
Jefferson City, MO 65102-7500

### MARY-KATE & ASHLEY SWEEPSTAKES

Name_____ (please print) _____

Address_____

City_____ State_____ Zip_____

Phone Number ( _____ ) _____

Age_____

**D**
**DUALSTAR**
**PUBLICATIONS**

No purchase necessary to enter.
Sweepstakes entries must be received by 4/15/97.

# The Adventures of Mary-Kate & Ashley™ Hollywood Sweepstakes

## OFFICIAL RULES:

1. No purchase necessary.

2. To enter, complete this official entry form or hand print your name, address, day and evening phone numbers along with the words "The Adventures of Mary-Kate & Ashley™ Hollywood Sweepstakes" on a 3" X 5" card and mail to The Adventures of Mary-Kate & Ashley™ Hollywood Sweepstakes, c/o Scholastic Trade Marketing Dept., P.O. Box 7500, Jefferson City, MO 65102-7500. Enter as often as you wish, but each entry must be mailed separately. One entry per envelope. Partially completed, illegible or mechanically reproduced entries will not be accepted. All entries must be received no later than April 15, 1997. Sponsors not responsible for delayed, damaged, lost, late, misdirected, incomplete, postage due mail, or illegible entries. All entries become the property of Scholastic, Inc. and will not be returned.

3. Sweepstakes open to U.S. residents who are between the ages of five and twelve years old by April 30, 1997, excluding employees of Scholastic Inc., Parachute Press, Inc., Warner Vision Entertainment Inc., Dualstar Entertainment Group, Inc., and their respective parent companies, affiliates, subsidiaries, advertising, promotion and fulfillment agencies, and the persons with whom each of the above are domiciled. Sweepstakes is void where prohibited by law.

4. One (1) Grand Prize winner will receive a Hollywood Weekend Adventure for a family of four to Hollywood, California. Trip includes: round trip coach airfare from airport nearest winner's home to Los Angeles airport; hotel accommodations for two (2) nights (1 double room); mid-sized rental car (eligible drivers only); $500 spending money, and ice cream party with Mary-Kate & Ashley Olsen. (Estimated retail value $3000). Grand Prize winners must utilize prize within one year from day of notification. Travel must include Saturday night stay. Date of trip to be decided by Dualstar Entertainment Group, Inc.

5. Odds of winning depend on total number of entries received. All prizes will be awarded. Winners will be selected in a random drawing on or about April 30, 1997, by Scholastic Inc., whose decisions are final. Winners will be notified by mail. Winners will be required to complete an affidavit of eligibility. Grand Prize winners and their guests must sign and return a liability and publicity release within 14 days of receipt. By acceptance of their prize, winners consent to the use of their names and photographs or likenesses by Scholastic Inc., Parachute Press, Inc., Dualstar Entertainment Group, Inc. and for publicity purposes without further compensation except where prohibited.

6. Only one prize will be awarded per individual, family, or household. Prizes are non-transferable, non-returnable, and cannot be sold or redeemed for cash. No substitutions allowed. Any federal, state, and local taxes on prizes are the sole responsibility of the winner. All federal, state, and local laws apply.

7. For a list of winners or a complete set of rules, send a self-addressed stamped envelope (excluding residents of Vermont and Washington) after April 30, 1997 to The Adventures of Mary-Kate & Ashley™ Hollywood Sweepstakes Winners List, c/o Scholastic Trade Marketing Dept., P.O. Box 7500, Jefferson City, MO 65102-7500.

# High-Falootin' Fun for the Whole Family!

## OWN IT ON VIDEO!

It doesn't matter if you live around the corner...
or around the world...
If you are a fan of Mary-Kate and Ashley Olsen,
you should be a member of

# MARY-KATE + ASHLEY'S FUN CLUB™

Here's what you get:
**Our Funzine**™
An autographed color photo
Two black & white individual photos
A full size color poster
An official **Fun Club**™ membership card
A **Fun Club**™ school folder
Two special **Fun Club**™ surprises
A holiday card
**Fun Club**™ collectibles catalog
Plus a **Fun Club**™ box to keep everything in

To join Mary-Kate + Ashley's Fun Club™, fill out the form
below and send it along with

U.S. Residents – $17.00
Canadian Residents – $22 U.S. Funds
International Residents – $27 U.S. Funds

**MARY-KATE + ASHLEY'S FUN CLUB**™
**859 HOLLYWOOD WAY, SUITE 275**
**BURBANK, CA 91505**

NAME:_____

ADDRESS:_____

CITY:_____STATE:_____ZIP:_____

PHONE: (____) _____BIRTHDATE:_____